BALZER + BRAY

PRE

BLUE

TOM SU

IMPRINT OF **HARPERCOLLINS***PUBLISHERS*

Have you heard the news?

Blue is the best color.

Nice try, but everyone knows

that yellow is the best color.

Look up and see for yourself—

blue is the color of the whole sky.

That's funny—all I see

is a bright yellow sun.

Well, blue is the only color
that has its own music.

Sure, but the instruments
are yellow.

And if you're blue,

it means you're sad.

So what? If you're yellow,

it means you're a scaredy-cat.

Speaking of cats, the *FASTEST*

animal in the world is yellow!

But the **BIGGEST**

animal in the world is blue!

And to top it off,

all the best food is blue.

BLUE FOOD

BLUEBERRIES · SLUSH
COTTON CANDY
POPSICLES · GUMMIES

I'm not sure I'd even consider

most of that food. . . .

Yellow food is MUCH better.

Plus, there are yellow birds, bugs, bikes, and all sorts of things.

Those can all be blue, too!

Well, the coolest cars are yellow.

Don't forget about big blue trucks!

WHOA!

What happened?

We're . . .

we're *green*.

WOW!

Look at all the cool stuff

we can both be!

Okay, truce.

Blue and yellow are the best . . .

TOGETHER!

Umm . . . excuse me?

I think everyone can agree:

Red is the best color of all time.

Hands down.

To infinity.

BLUE
vs.
YELLOW
vs.
RED

the end

for kelly

Balzer + Bray is an imprint of HarperCollins Publishers.
Blue vs. Yellow
Copyright © 2017 by Tom Sullivan

ISBN 978-0-06-245295-5

The artist used Sharpies and Photoshop to create
the illustrations for this book.
Typography by Tom Sullivan
17 18 19 20 21 SCP 10 9 8 7 6 5 4 3 2 1
❖
First Edition